# Salmon's Journey

## and More Northwest Coast Stories

Learning From Nature and the World Around Us

**Stories and Illustrations**

# Robert James Challenger

Copyright © 2001 Robert James Challenger

National Library of Canada Cataloguing in Publication Data

Challenger, Robert James, 1953-

Salmon's Journey and More Northwest Coast Stories

ISBN 1-894384-34-2

1. Nature stories, Canadian (English)* 2. Children's stories, Canadian (English)* I. Title.

PS8555.H277S24 2001      jC813'.54      C2001-911230-0
PZ7.C3498SA 2001

First Edition 2001

Heritage House acknowledges the financial support of the Government of Canada through the Book Publishing Industry Development Program (BPIDP), Canada Council for the Arts, and the British Columbia Arts Council for our publishing activities.

Cover and book design by Darlene Nickull
Edited by Rhonda Bailey

HERITAGE HOUSE PUBLISHING COMPANY LTD.
Unit #108 - 17665 66 A Ave., Surrey, B.C. V3S 2A7

Printed in Canada

This book is dedicated to my Mom,
Jean Challenger,
who has put feet to the words,
"Life is what you make it."

# Other Books by Robert James Challenger

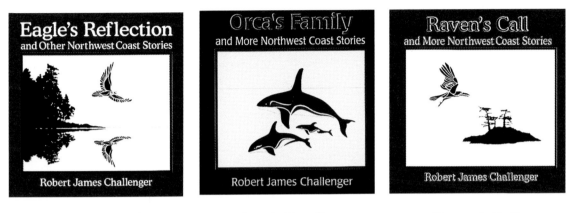

### Eagle's Reflection
and Other Northwest
Coast Stories
ISBN 1-895811-07-4
$9.95

### Orca's Family
and More Northwest
Coast Stories
ISBN 1-895811-39-2
$9.95

### Raven's Call
and More Northwest
Coast Stories
ISBN 1-895811-91-0
$9.95

*Wonderful Northwest Coast stories for kids ... Jim Challenger is a real artist a his book demonstrates.*
　　　　　　—Shaw Cable's "What's Happening?"

*Modern day fables are the right length. ... knows how to write for the oral storyteller; the written words slip easily off the tongue.*
　　　　　　—Times Colonist

*Clear images ... brief, narrative style will appeal to young readers. Appropriate for read-aloud, ... use the moral content to promote family values.*
　　　　　　—Resource Links

*Each story would make perfect bedtime reading.*
　　　　　　—Vancouver Sun.

*Challenger's prose bears a deliberate resemblance to First Nation oral traditions: human and nature interact freely, and both are capable of folly, repentance, and wisdom. In his artwork, Challenger also embraces West Coast aboriginal culture by portraying his characters in exquisite Haida-style prints ... returning to the stories is like returning to a favorite restaurant even after you have long ago memorized the menu. Highly recommended.*
　　　　　　—Canadian Book Review Annual

# Contents

# Salmon's Journey

The little creek was bright with fish swimming through the shallows and searching for a place to lay their eggs. It was fall, and Sockeye Salmon had returned to the very stretch of creek where she was born. It had been a long journey, full of adventures.

In the first year, Sockeye Salmon emerged from her egg beneath the gravel and made her way to the surface. For the first while she hid in the shallow waters along the stream bank to stay away from the bigger fish and the birds. When she was a few months old, she and all the other newborns began their journey down the river towards the sea. It was spring, and as the sun shone brightly, Sockeye Salmon's color became shining silver.

She stayed together with the others in a large school, for she knew that they would be safer if they kept together. Drawn by instinct she began a long journey out into the deep ocean. At first, she ate the little shrimp and plankton that drifted in the currents. As she grew, she began to feast on the herring and anchovies. Sockeye Salmon became larger and stronger every day. She practised swimming and became one of the fastest in her school.

That was a good thing, because she had some close calls. Once she was chased by Sea Lion and another time by Orca. Both times she just managed to escape their snapping jaws.

One day she felt the urge to turn around and start back towards her birthplace. As she swam closer to the river she started to smell the fresh water. Mixed in was the unmistakable scent of the water that came from her own spawning creek.

The battle up the river was hard. The rushing water battered her against the stones, and the rapids and waterfalls used up much of her energy. Luckily Sockeye Salmon's years of swimming in the ocean had prepared her for this part of the journey.

As the days grew shorter, Sockeye Salmon began to turn red, like the glow of the autumn sunsets. This bright red colour was a sign that her life was now nearing its most important time.

She turned off the main river into the small stream where she had been born. She dug her nest and, with her mate by her side, laid her eggs into the gravel. It was the end of her journey.

It was time for the next generation to begin their journey through life.

# Red Snapper's Colour

Grandmother and her young granddaughter sat near their campfire, watching the flames flicker into the night sky. Sparks scooted around above the fire, leaving traces of light as they went. The light from the campfire cast a warm orange glow over their faces.

Grandmother noticed the girl staring at her and asked, "What do you see in my face that is so fascinating to you?"

The girl replied, "I was just looking at you and wondering what you looked like when you were my age."

Grandmother asked, "What do you think I looked like?"

"Well," the girl said, "I guess you didn't have all those wrinkles and your hair wasn't so grey."

Grandmother smiled. "You're right. But why are you wondering about what I looked like?"

Her granddaughter replied, "Because I was wondering about what I will look like when I am older, like you."

"You will look different than you do now. It's just like Red Snapper, who lives deep in the ocean. Red Snappers live many years, just like us. Every sunset makes their scales turn a little deeper orange, and every day that they learn something new another scale grows.

"By the time Red Snapper is grown up he is the colour of the campfire's glowing red coals and has thousands of scales all over his body.

"Every experience you have makes you change. The days you spend enjoying life will show as wrinkles in your skin, and the challenges that you overcome you will see as grey in your hair," said Grandmother.

"But, with age comes a lifetime of sunsets you got to enjoy and lots of pleasant memories of lessons you learned along the way."

# Hermit Crab's Home

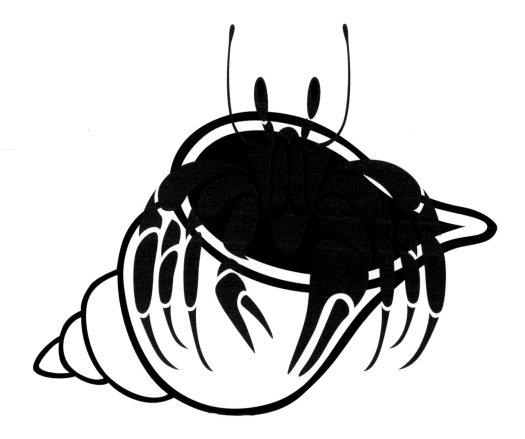

The last box of clothes was carried out of the house. Now it was empty and the small boy wandered through the rooms that echoed with the sound of his steps.

It seemed so different from the home he had grown up in his whole life. He sat down on the bottom step of the stairway and began to cry.

Father heard him and came down the stairs and sat beside him. He didn't have to ask why the boy was crying. He knew, because he too felt the same sadness at leaving their house.

But Father remembered a story Grandfather had told him.

He took his son's hand and said to him, "At the beach, Hermit Crab lives in the empty shell of a snail. When Hermit Crab was young he found a pretty white shell that he could fit comfortably inside. It wasn't too big for his small legs to carry. It was the perfect home.

"But as he grew, his home began to get too small for him. He spent many days searching and eventually he found a larger, brown snail shell to be his house. Reluctantly, he crawled out of his old white shell and into his new brown one.

"His old home lay empty on the sand. He was sad to leave his pretty white shell behind.

"'But,' Hermit Crab said to himself, 'this new brown one is really very nice and gives me more room to grow. I'm already beginning to feel like it's my home.'"

Father said to his son, "Our family is like Hermit Crab. We've outgrown this house and we need to move to one that fits us better."

"But I like having our home in this house." said the boy.

Father replied, "Once we are at our new house and all our things are put away, you'll find it becomes a home just like this place is. You'll discover, just like Hermit Crab did, that home is more about who is living in a house than about what it looks like."

# Why Halibut Looks Up

The rain, carried by the gusts of wind, blew through the trees of the forest. Large, cold drops fell from the branches and soaked the ground. It was late afternoon and already the light was fading. The forest seemed dark and desolate.

A girl sat by the kitchen window, her face pressed against the cold glass, watching. She turned to Grandmother and said, "I feel so sad when it's gloomy and dark outside."

Grandmother replied, "You need to cheer up. You know the cold and darkness doesn't last forever. "

"It seems to last forever to me," said the small girl.

Grandmother, who was just removing a batch of cookies from the oven, came over to the window, put her arm around the child, and said, "Let me tell you a story that will help to cheer you up.

"Many years ago there was a big fish that lived in the ocean. Its name was Halibut. Halibut swam about in the deepest part of the ocean where it was always cold and dark.

"In those days Halibut had big eyes on either side of its head so it was always looking into the darkness of the ocean.

"One day Halibut was chasing some little fish, and they led him up near the surface of the ocean.

"It was a summer day and the light and warmth delighted Halibut. It was wonderful to feel the heat of the sun and to see everything in such bright colour.

"Halibut was amazed that he had been swimming around for years, feeling so depressed, without ever looking up to see the brightness that was right above him.

"Halibut liked looking at the bright surface so much that now his eyes have moved to the top of his head so he is always looking up. He just ignores the gloom and darkness around him."

Grandmother looked at the child and said, "So, perhaps you should be like Halibut. Look at the brighter side of things around you and choose to ignore the things that make you sad."

The child looked up at her and smiled.

"You're right, Grandmother. I am looking around me and I see those cookies you just baked. I already feel better!"

# Clam's Shell

The tide was out, and the vast stretch of flat sand in front of the village was exposed. Grandmother walked barefoot along the beach as the children ran around her.

One of the youngest let out a yelp of surprise.

"Grandmother!" she said, "Clam just squirted water all over me!"

Grandmother smiled and replied, "Come over here and I'll tell you about what Clam is trying to tell you."

As they walked along on the warm sand, Grandmother said, "Many years ago, when my great- grandmother was a child, there was another child who was born into the village. This child was different from all the rest.

"The boy was very smart and among all the children, he was the first to walk and the first to talk. But he looked different from the rest because had been born with a mark on his forehead, a mark shaped like the new moon.

"The children in the village didn't understand what the mark meant, It scared them. They started to be mean to the boy, to not let him take part in their games.

"The boy became lonely and quiet. The others continued to make fun of him so much that one stormy day the boy was so sad he ran into the ocean. The winter waves picked him up and swept him away.

"Eagle swept down. With a touch of her wing, she transformed the boy into Clam.

"Eagle said to Clam, 'I have given you a hard shell to protect you from the world. Now you can live in peace, without anyone to bother you.'"

Grandmother pointed to a hole in the sand, "So, to this day, Clam still lives beneath the sand. If you get too close to him he squirts water at you to remind you that it isn't right to be mean to others just because they look different from you."

# Kokanee's Sparkle

**A** whisper of wind swept down from the green meadows and across the surface of the lake. As it brushed over the surface of the water small waves rippled. The sun, high in the summer sky, reflected off the small waves like a million sparkling stars.

Two brothers sat in their boat and let the quiet of the forest lake blanket them. The two normally had busy lives, caring for their families and working to earn a living. But each year they took time and travelled back to fish on this lake and to enjoy the peaceful quiet of nature together.

The older brother taught his younger brother how to tie on the fly hooks to match the insects that the trout were feeding on that day. He taught him to look around him and watch for the insects rising from the lake. He told him their names and how to identify them at different stages of their lives.

The older brother showed the younger one how to cast the fly out across the water and how to bring it back in slowly.

"I like this lake," said the younger brother.

"Me too," said the older one. "I love the peaceful way it makes me feel and the warmth of the light reflecting off the water."

"What kind of fish live in this lake?" the younger one asked.

The older brother replied, "There are two kinds. One is called Rainbow Trout. He has a beautiful band of colour along his sides that he got from a rainbow that touched down on this lake at the end of a rainstorm.

"The other is a silver fish called Kokanee.

"Kokanee was once a dark-brown fish, but one day, a day just like this one, he was looking for food near the surface. He saw a fly just above him and he jumped out of the water to get it. As he splashed back down the sparkles on the water stuck to him, and he became bright silver.

"Kokanee had many children. When the young ones swam up creeks to other lakes they took the sparkles with them, and that's why all lakes have sparkling silver on their waves."

# Robin's Red Feathers

It was early morning, and the sun was just rising. Granddaughter sat on a large stone near the meadow and watched Robin. The early spring grass had come up from its winter hiding place beneath the old dried grass from last year.

Granddaughter watched as Robin hunted for worms to feed her nest full of babies in the old maple tree.

Robin would hop along the ground, stop and turn her head to the side, then hop along a bit more and stop again. Every once in a while Robin would peck a hole in the grass and pull out a worm. She would fly to her nest, feed it to her babies, then fly back down to the meadow and begin searching again. Back and forth she flew from the meadow to her nest.

The little girl called out to Robin, "How do you know when there is a worm under the grass if you can't see it?"

Robin replied, "I know they are there because I see the grass move as they crawl around under the roots."

"How did you learn that?" the little girl asked.

Robin replied, "Many years ago, after I hatched from my egg, my mother would feed my brothers, sisters, and me worms that she found in this meadow.

"When we were big enough to leave our nest she flew with us down to the grass to find worms for ourselves. From watching her, I thought it would be easy, but it wasn't.

"First, I tried looking for them. I hopped around for a long time, but I didn't see any worms.

"Next I tried listening for the worms. But, that didn't work, because the worms didn't make any sound.

"Then I tried digging for them. I pecked a lot of holes but never found a worm.

"As the sun was just rising, its bright light shone across the grass, and that's when I saw some grass moving. I hopped over, dug a hole, and found my first worm.

"As I sat eating I noticed that the light from the sunrise had turned the feathers on my chest this beautiful deep orange.

"Today, my feathers remind me that even though I have grown up, every day that the sun rises is another chance to learn something new."

# Starfish Becomes a Shining Light

**G**randmother and Granddaughter lay on their backs on top of the hill behind their home. Above them, spread like shells on a beach, lay a million stars.

It was summer and the warmth of the day just passed still surrounded them. They had spent the day together, and Grandmother had shown the child how to gather the blackberries from the vines that grew alongside the pond. She had shown her how to lift the vines with a stick to find the ripe berries that others had missed.

They had taken the berries home and Granddaughter had helped Grandmother turn the sweet berries into a rich jam that would last them through the next winter.

Now darkness had come, and they had gone for a walk up the hill to look at the summer stars.

Grandmother reached over, took Granddaughter's hand in hers, and gave it a squeeze.

Above them a flare of light streaked across the sky.

"What was that?" Granddaughter asked.

"That was a star, coming down to live here on earth with us," said Grandmother.

"Why is it coming here to live?" the girl asked.

Grandmother replied, "Somewhere, at the moment we saw that shooting star, a new baby was being born. That star's spirit became part of that little child. It will give the child a special energy to help it to learn from others who have gone before."

Granddaughter said, "Just like I learned about picking berries from you today."

"Yes," Grandmother replied, "You have a star's energy inside you that makes you want to learn from others."

The little girl thought about that for a moment then asked, "If the spirit of a star becomes part of a baby being born, what happens to the star?"

Grandmother replied, "The star sinks to the bottom of the ocean, where it becomes Starfish. It lives there with the other stars until it is time for its spirit to go back up into the sky to become a shining light for someone else's journey."

# Coyote's Friend

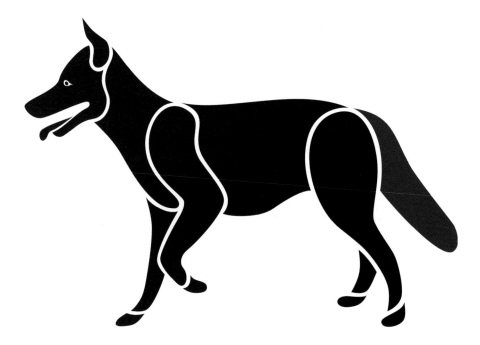

The warm, dry cabin was a good place to be on this wild winter day. Outside, the snow swirled around the trees and piled up against the shed in the yard.

Inside the cabin, a small boy sat in the warmth of his home and family and looked out the frosty window. He saw a movement off at the edge of the forest.

As he watched, Coyote emerged from the trees and walked across to the shed. He crawled into a sheltered spot, out of the wind and snow, and lay down to rest.

The boy called to Grandmother to come and see.

"Yes," she said, "I put up that shelter for him. When the weather is bad, like today, he likes to come and lie there. I leave a bucket of water for him to drink and if it's really cold, some food for him to take back to his family."

"Why do you do that?" asked the boy.

"As a way of saying thank you to Coyote. You see, many years ago, before we came to live here, Coyote had already lived in this place for many thousands of years. He had all the food and forest that he wanted.

"Where we came from, there were too many people and not enough to eat. We set out to look for a better life, and when we found this meadow in the forest we made it our new home.

"Coyote welcomed us and tried to be our friend. But we tried to force Coyote to move away so we could have the meadow all to ourselves."

"That was not really fair, Grandmother," said the boy.

"No, it wasn't," she said. "It would be like me coming to live at your house and telling you to leave, even though it was your home first.

"Sometimes we get so concerned about our own needs that we forget that the others living in this world also have needs.

"So, when I remembered that it was Coyote who first allowed me to come and live in the meadow, I knew that it was only right for me to be his friend and help him to live here too."

# Porcupine's Lesson

The older boy and his friend were playing happily together. They climbed up the hill above the beach, where Eagle's nest sat in the old fir tree. They pretended to be explorers discovering a new land. They planted a flag and named the new country.

The older boy declared, "I name this My Land, and all that I see is now mine."

"Wait a second," the younger boy said. "Shouldn't it be Our Land, since we found it together?"

"No, I'm the oldest and strongest so it's My Land. I'm going to build a fence to keep everyone out, including you," he replied.

The younger boy tried to pull down the flag but the older one punched him until he cried. The younger boy ran back down the path with tears streaming down his face.

The older boy sat at the top of his hill. As he watched, Porcupine came up the path.

Porcupine asked, "Why was that other boy crying?"

The older boy replied, "I hit him because I wanted to call this My Land and not allow him inside my fence."

Porcupine said to him, "The land cannot belong to you any more than air or water can belong to you.

"The land isn't anyone's to own. We all need land to live on, just like we need water to drink and air to breathe.

"My sharp quills protect me like a fence, but they also keep others who could be my friends away, because they are afraid they might get hurt if they try to come too close.

"Trust me when I say it's not a good idea to put up fences between you and your friends. In the end, you'll have the protection of your fence, but you'll be all by yourself."

"Thank you Porcupine," said the boy. "I'll go catch up to my friend and tell him that we can share this land together, and I won't try to keep everyone out."

# Sea Otter's Favour

Grandfather sat fishing from his boat as it drifted alongside the forest of kelp growing in the shallow waters beside the reef.

He watched all the creatures who lived in this underwater forest.

Heron and Seagull walked along the floating tops of the kelp and looked for little fish among the swaying fronds that streamed out in the gentle current.

Deeper down, big fish hid in the cool shade of the kelp, which gripped the dark bottom and stretched up to the light above.

Grandfather needed to catch one of the fish to take home for his family's dinner, but he wasn't able to coax them out of the kelp to bite on his fishing line.

Sea Otter saw him and asked, "Do you need some help, Grandfather?"

"I sure do," he replied. "If I don't catch a fish soon, my family will all be going to bed hungry tonight."

Sea Otter remembered the time she had been hungry and Grandfather had shared some of the clams he had dug. Now she had the opportunity to return his kindness.

Sea Otter dived below the kelp and chased the big fish out towards Grandfather. She sped after one of them and chased it right up out of the water and into Grandfather's boat.

Sea Otter looked up at Grandfather and they both laughed.

"That's certainly a different way of catching fish than I'm used to," he said.

Sea Otter dove back into the ocean.

Grandfather waved to her and called, "Thank you. Because of you my family won't go hungry this evening."

Sea Otter replied, "I'm glad that I could do something nice for you, just like you did for me when you had the chance."

# Snow Bear's Mistake

**A** boy and his father hiked homewards along the pathway. The snow from the night before had covered the trees with a thick white blanket. It was unusually quiet, and their voices were muffled by the deep snow. Most creatures had retreated to the shelter of caves and the old-growth forest.

All of a sudden the snow slid off a tree's branches and cascaded to the ground beside them in a shower of ice crystals.

Father said, "Snow Bear's spirit must have pushed the snow off that tree. I see he still hasn't learned his lesson."

The son asked, "What lesson is that?"

As they walked along, Father told his son the story of Snow Bear.

"Thousands of years ago Snow Bear lived way up the valley from here. He was pure white and liked to live high up in the mountains where the snow drifts lasted throughout the summer. He could blend in and not be seen when he went out looking for food.

"He wanted to go down in the valley too, so one day he pushed one of the snowdrifts towards the valley bottom. The moving snow became a glacier, sliding down the mountain, crushing everything in its path.

"The trouble was, that once a glacier starts, it is impossible to stop. In a short time it reached the valley, and all the animals and plants that lived there were destroyed. Now, Snow Bear had nothing to eat. He travelled ahead of the glacier to this place where we are now. This was the last place that the glacier covered. When the glacier came, Snow Bear disappeared just like all the other plants and animals.

"The ice is gone now but we can still learn from what happened to Snow Bear. Sometimes we start things for our own greedy reasons, but those things often get out of control and do a lot of harm to others and to ourselves.

"We need to remember that when we don't respect nature's way, it always catches up to us in the end."

# Seagull Saves the Day

Grandfather pulled his hat down tight on his head to keep it from blowing away in the strong winter wind. He held tightly to the tiller of his boat as it was thrown before the storm's waves. It had been hours since he had last seen land, and in the swirling rain and cloud, he had lost all sense of direction.

He looked at Grandson, who was huddled under a blanket in the bow of the boat, and in a tense voice said, "Looks like I've got us into a lot of trouble. I've lost my way. I don't know if I'm sailing towards land or farther out to sea."

Grandson replied, "I'm sure we'll find a way if we try, Grandfather."

Grandfather sighed and said, "It's no use trying. There's no way we'll ever find our way back."

"Well," Grandson said, "I remember one time when I was fishing out off the point and the fog rolled in. I knew that I wasn't far from land, but in the fog I couldn't see which way to paddle. As I sat worrying about which way to go I heard Seagull calling to me from the beach. I just followed the sound of her call until I could see the shore again."

"That was a good idea, but with this wind howling around our ears it is impossible to hear Seagull's call today," Grandfather said.

Grandson watched the whitecaps' foam on top of the waves. He saw the wind pick up the foam and blow it high into the sky. It gave him an idea.

He said to Grandfather, "Well, if we can't hear Seagull, maybe we can see her and follow her back to land."

They began to look around for any sign of Seagull flying by.

Suddenly, a whitecap on a nearby wave blew up into the air and became a white bird. It was Seagull.

She circled their boat and flew off in the opposite direction. Grandfather quickly turned the boat around and followed her. Within a couple of hours they could see the coastline again and were able to sail into the safety of the bay.

As they tied up their boat to the wharf, Grandfather said to Grandson, "Thank you. Today it was you and Seagull who taught me a lesson. I was ready to give up, but you two showed me that for every problem there's always a solution, if I just don't give up trying."

# How Dragonfly Flies

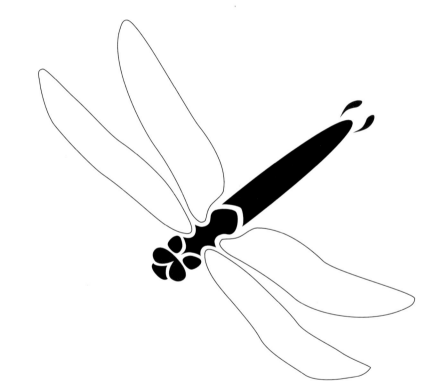

**G**randfather watched his young grandson as he ran about the meadow playing with the other children in a game of tag. He had picked an older boy and was chasing him, even though it was clear to Grandfather that the other child was a much faster runner than his grandson was.

Finally the younger boy came over and flopped down on the cool grass beside Grandfather.

"I'm tired of this game," he said. "I can never catch the other person so I'm always the one who is chasing. I never get to be the one someone else has to chase."

Grandfather smiled at him and said, "Let me tell you the story of Dragonfly, and perhaps you can use his lesson in your game.

"Dragonfly, many years ago, had a similar problem to yours. He loved to eat small flying insects, but they were very hard to catch.

"He would see one and spend the whole day chasing it around. Most times he never did catch it.

"One day, Eagle said to him, 'You need to be smart enough to know which things are worth chasing and which things are not. Look around as you fly and take advantage of the things that come to you, rather than wasting your energy chasing things that are trying to get away.'"

Grandfather pointed at Dragonfly, who was hovering over near the trees.

"That is why Dragonfly likes to stay in one place and let the wind bring the insects to him. When they get close he simply darts to one side, and they are his."

Grandfather put his hand on the young boy's shoulder and said, "In your game you need to be able to see that some of the other children can run faster than you and ignore them. Wait for the ones who run close to you, and then quickly go after them."

Grandson ran off to play again. He called back, "Thanks, Grandfather. I'll try to be more like Dragonfly and take advantage of the things that come to me."

# Grasshopper's Strength

The hot summer sun beat down on the dirt road, where two boys walked along, kicking up little clouds of dust with each footstep.

Grasshopper jumped from the dry grass onto the road in front of them.

He asked them, "Where are you going?"

The bigger boy replied, "We are going to the lake down in the valley for a swim."

The smaller one said, "I'm going to swim all the way across the lake today."

The bigger boy turned to the smaller one, "Don't be stupid. I'm way bigger than you, and even I can't swim that far."

Grasshopper said to the bigger boy, "So, you think that size is the only measure of strength. How about if we have a race to the lake—you against me—to see if size is all that matters?"

"OK," said the bigger boy.

The two of them lined up and the smaller boy counted, "One, two, three … go!"

The bigger boy took off running, with Grasshopper jumping along just behind him.

On the flat road, the older boy could go faster than Grasshopper, but when they turned off the road onto the pathway down to the lake it was a different story.

Grasshopper was small, so he could get under the branches that hung low over the path. The bigger boy had to slow down to get under them.

And when they got to a steep part of the path that was covered in boulders, Grasshopper used his jumping skill to leap over the rocks. The bigger boy had to climb over each one.

Grasshopper was already there, waiting for him, when the bigger boy reached the lake.

The boy sat down, gasping for air, too tired to even speak.

A few minutes later the smaller boy caught up to the two of them.

Grasshopper said to the smaller boy, "You see, being bigger doesn't always mean being better.

"If you are trying to pick apples from a tall tree, then being bigger is good. But, as I have shown your friend just now, if you are trying to run down a hill covered in trees and rocks, then being small, and a good jumper, is best."

# Flowers for Honeybee

The flower blossoms in Grandmother's garden carpeted her back yard. Every corner was bursting with bright-coloured blooms, and the fragrance of the flowers filled the summer air.

Grandmother walked through her garden with her granddaughter.

Grandmother said to her, "There are lots of flowers this year, so let's pick a nice bouquet for your mother. We'll surprise her with it when she comes home."

As they picked the flowers, Granddaughter asked, "How come you plant so many flowers in your garden, Grandmother?"

Grandmother smiled and said, "Sit down here on the bench, and I'll tell you the story of Honeybee. Then I think you'll have the answer to your question."

Grandmother took the child's hand and said to her, "Over there, in the corner of the garden, is a beehive that Grandfather built. Inside it, Honeybee can raise her family, safely away from animals that might harm them.

"In this world, Honeybee's job is to fly from one flower to the next, spreading the flowers' pollen so their seeds can become new flowers next year.

"As thanks, each of the flowers gives Honeybee some of its nectar. Back at the hive, Honeybee turns that nectar into honey. If she has more honey than she needs, she shares it with you and me so we can enjoy its sweetness too. Then, if we have some honey left over I trade it to other people for flower seeds to plant in my garden.

"Now, if there weren't enough flowers in my garden, then Honeybee's family would not have enough to eat, and there would be no honey to share with me. Without that honey, I wouldn't have anything to trade for seeds, so the next year there would be even fewer flowers and less honey. Within a few years all the flowers and Honeybee could be gone.

"So, that's why every year I try to plant more flowers for Honeybee to visit. That way there will always be enough honey for all of us to enjoy."

Grandmother smiled at Granddaughter and said, "So, here's the answer to your question why my garden has so many flowers."

"The more nice things that I do for Honeybee, the more nice things Honeybee does for me. And, the more that Honeybee does for me, the more I can do for Honeybee!"

# Being Kind to Snake

**S**nake sat sleeping on a large, flat stone, warming his body in the sunshine. It had been a long winter. He was happy that it was springtime, and things were beginning to get warmer.

Two boys came up the pathway toward where he lay. The younger of the two boys saw Snake, picked up a stick, and ran towards him.

The older boy called out, "What are you doing?"

The boy replied, "Snake is bad. He is poisonous and his bite can kill us. I'm going to kill Snake with this stick."

Snake woke up and saw the boy running towards him. He saw the stick and started to slither off to the protection of his den under the stone.

The older boy shouted at the younger one, "Stop! Before you hurt Snake, let me ask you something."

The boy with the stick stopped and said, "What's your question?"

The older boy asked, "Have you, or anyone you know, ever been bitten by Snake?"

The other boy thought for a moment, then lowered the stick and said, "No."

The older boy asked, "Then why do you think this one's bite is poisonous?

"Well," the younger one replied, "He's long, has shiny skin, and is the same colour as the ones I've seen pictures of that are poisonous."

The older boy said, "So you think just because they look similar that they are all dangerous?"

The younger boy thought about that, then replied, "I guess so."

The older boy said to him, "Well, you are wrong. Snake who has his home here is harmless to us. He has no fangs or poison to hurt us. All he wants to do is live and raise his family here."

The young boy looked at Snake and said, "Sorry if I scared you."

He dropped the stick, and the two boys continued up the path, leaving Snake to lie peacefully in the sunshine.

The older boy put his hand on the younger boy's shoulder and said to him, "Remember, you can't judge something by what it looks like. Snake is just like people. Just because one person is bad, it doesn't mean that everyone who looks like that person is also bad. "

# Wolf Learns to Fish

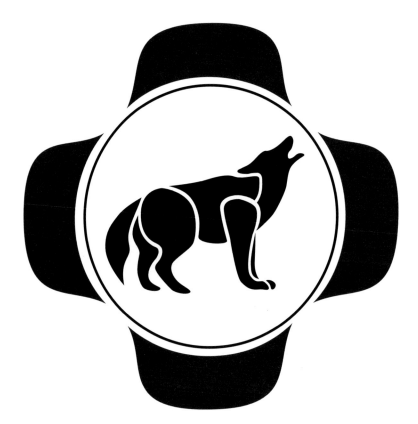

**W**olf emerged from her den, followed closely behind by her litter of newborn pups. Their eyes took a moment to adjust from the darkness of their birthplace to the bright spring sunshine.

In the warm days that followed she showed them how to hunt in the rocks at the base of the mountain. She took them to the spots she knew where there was lush grass and clean water. She taught them to stay away from bigger animals that could harm them.

One day, in the fall of their first year, she took them down to the river to show them how to catch fish. She rushed into the water and chased around and around. The fish swam in all directions, but finally she caught a very small one. Panting hard from her running about, she brought the little fish over to the bank where her pups were watching.

She said to them, "Now, each of you go and catch a fish for yourself."

Soon the river was a riot of splashing wolf pups and leaping fish as the puppies rushed about.

One pup got tired, and so, to catch his breath, he stopped running. As he stood there, very still, a big fish swam up without seeing him. The pup just reached down and caught it as it swam right under his nose.

He took the fish over to his mother and said, "Look at the big fish I caught. Instead of doing it your way, I just stood still and the fish came to me."

Wolf said to him, "Well, that's not the right way to catch fish. You need to do it my way, by chasing them, the way my mother showed me when I was your age."

But, one of the other pups had seen her brother catch the big fish, so she tried standing still too. In no time she had also caught one. Soon all the pups were using the new way of catching fish.

Wolf just stood on the bank and howled at them to do it her way.

Then, from the tree above the riverbank, Wolf heard Eagle laughing at her.

Eagle called down, "Looks like your young ones have taught you something today instead of the other way around."

Wolf had to laugh. "Yes, I have to admit that they seem to have found a better way to catch fish," she said.

Eagle said to her, "I'm glad you are willing to change. It's important for parents to remember that just because we have always done something one way doesn't mean our children can't show us a better way of doing it today."

# Eagle's Spirit

The old man was very sick, and soon his time in this world would be finished. His family gathered at his side to help him through this part of his life's journey.

His great-grandchild put her tiny, soft hand into his rough, time-worn hand. As he held it, she said to him, "Great-Grandfather, when we die, where do we go?"

Great-Grandfather smiled at her and said, "There are two answers to that question, because each life is made up of two parts.

"The first part of life is the body that we live within.

"All through my life I have gathered the energy around me into this body. The energy came from the food that I ate, the water that I drank, and from the love that you and the rest of my family gave to me.

"Now, it is time for me to give that energy back to the world so it can be used by little ones, like you, who are still growing and need it.

The little girl asked, "What is the other part of life, Great-Grandfather?"

"The second part is the spirit that each of us has inside us," he said.

"I believe that spirit lives on, even after the body it once lived in is gone. The spirit gets to choose to live wherever it wants."

"What about you, Great-Grandfather?" the child asked. "Where is your spirit going to live?"

"I have always admired Eagle, so I think that is what I will choose to become," he said. "That way I can live in the old fir tree behind the house and watch over you as you grow up."

"I'll be sad after you are gone," his great-grandchild said. "You've always been here to listen to me when I need someone to talk to."

He replied, "You don't need to be sad. If you miss seeing me you will just need to look in your memories to see my face again. And if you miss talking to me, just look up and I'll be waiting at the top of the old fir tree, ready to listen to you."

# Why Jellyfish Never Stops

On a hot summer day Grandmother walked along the beach with her great-grandson. The tide was low, exposing a wide expanse of warm sand before them. A gentle breeze blew in off the sea, and above them, Eagle soared in the rising air currents.

Great-Grandson turned around and looked at their footprints, which trailed far off into the distance behind them.

He said, "It looks like we've been walking forever, Grandmother. I don't know if I'll be strong enough to get to the other end of the beach and back again."

Grandmother smiled at him and replied, "Well, if I can make it at my age, then you can on your young legs."

Great-Grandson said to her, "How old are you, Grandmother?"

Grandmother replied, " I have been seventy-eight years in this world, although it seems like only yesterday that I was a child your age, walking along this beach with my grandmother. She used to tell me to think like Jellyfish when I had a long journey to take.

"Jellyfish lives out in the ocean and although she swims very slowly, she swims all the time. Every time she pulses, she travels a little bit farther.

"Although sometimes the current pushes against her, she keeps swimming so she doesn't get pushed too far back. Jellyfish knows that for every current that pushes, eventually the tide will change and the same current will carry her forward.

"So, Great-Grandson, although your steps are small, if you keep walking you'll be able to get back home without too much trouble."

Great-Grandson looked up at her and smiled.

"All right, Grandmother," he said. "I'll be like Jellyfish and keep on going."

Grandmother smiled back at him and said, "That's good, because there are lots of things to gain from not giving up when things look tough.

"Look at me. Although I've had times in my lifetime when I seemed to be going backwards, I've always kept trying. Because of that I've been able to enjoy getting older. I have seen my children grow up, and my grandchildren too. I have even been able to see you, my great-grandson, start on your journey."

# Fir Tree's Seed

As the spring sun warmed a cone hanging high up in a fir tree, the cone ripened and turned from green to golden brown. Squirrel, who was out looking for food, nipped the cone off the branch and let it fall towards the ground. As it fell, one seed escaped from it, and thus began a new tree's long journey through life.

The seed's wing made it flutter as it fell. Caught by a gust of wind, it blew across the meadow to the wet area near the pond's edge and came to rest on a patch of fresh soil.

That night, a gentle rain fell, and the seed was covered with a light layer of earth. Water and warmth helped it to sprout, and as spring came, a seedling poked up out of the dirt into the sunshine.

The seedling began to gather energy from the sun, soil, and water. The little tree was so small it could hide under the tall grass so that Deer didn't see it when she was looking for something to eat.

Each year the tree grew a bit taller and its trunk and bark became a bit thicker. Below ground, its roots wound through the soil to look for nutrients and water and anchored the growing tree against the strong winter winds.

When Fir Tree was about forty years old, Raven came and built her nest on one of its strong branches. Each year Raven returned to the same nest in Fir Tree to raise her young.

For hundreds of years Fir Tree continued to grow. One winter, a fierce wind snapped its top off, but Eagle came and built her nest there and she too used Fir Tree as her home.

As Fir Tree became very old, Woodpecker came and drilled holes into the bark to hollow out a home inside the tree. She raised her young there until one winter when a windstorm came and Fir Tree finally fell with a great crash to the ground below.

In the moisture of the forest floor, Fir Tree quickly became covered in moss. The wood rotted and released nutrients that it had gathered through many years back into the soil.

A few hundred feet away, a cone on another tree released a seed that fluttered towards the ground where old Fir Tree lay, and another cycle of life began.

# About the Author

Born in Vancouver, B.C. in 1953, Robert James (Jim) Challenger has lived all of his life near the rugged Pacific coast. He is the son of proud fourth generation Canadians who raise their children to appreciate nature and the lessons that can be learned from it.

Jim spent his childhood summers on Thetis Island where he began to study and appreciate the unique wildlife, fish and birds that inhabit the Pacific Northwest and B.C. west coast. Moving to Victoria, B.C. in 1973, Jim met his wife Joannie, a school teacher, and they built their home among the evergreens near the Strait of Juan de Fuca. They have two daughters, Kristi and Kari.

In this peaceful coastal setting, with the majesty of the Olympic Peninsula on the horizon, Jim's artistic side flourished. A strong admirer of historic First Nation and Native American art and legends, he began designing his own images. Jim developed a special process to carve his designs into the rounded stones found on the windswept beaches of the Pacific. Patrons worldwide have enjoyed not only Jim's beautiful carvings but also the stories that inspired them. His stone carvings are owned by collectors across Canada, Japan, Europe, South America and the United States.

With the images to inspire him, he created a collection of fables that his daughters and their grandparents might enjoy. In 1995 the first collection of his work was successfully published as *Eagle's Reflection and Other Northwest Coast Stories* (ISBN 1-895811-07-4) followed by *Orca's Family and More Northwest Coast Stories* (ISBN 1-895811-39-2) in 1997 and *Raven's Call and More Northwest Coast Stories* (ISBN 1-89581-91-0) in 1999.

Jim's stories bring a unique perspective to lessons we can learn from nature and the world around us. They are stories that are meant to be shared and enjoyed among family and friends.